You Are A

SUPERHERO

written by
Lauren Grabois Fischer

pictures by
Devin Hunt

The
Be
Books

www.TheBEbooks.com

D1401630

Published by The BE Books

www.TheBEbooks.com

@theBEbooks

Dedication Page

This book is dedicated to my husband, Michael,

who is a real life superhero. You truly are the best husband and father.

I am so grateful to have you in my life. Thank you for choosing me.

I dedicate this book to all of the real life superheroes out there.

You are making a positive change in this world.

Keep it up. You are exactly where you are supposed to be.

You wake up each day
with a choice;

SMILE

Or frown

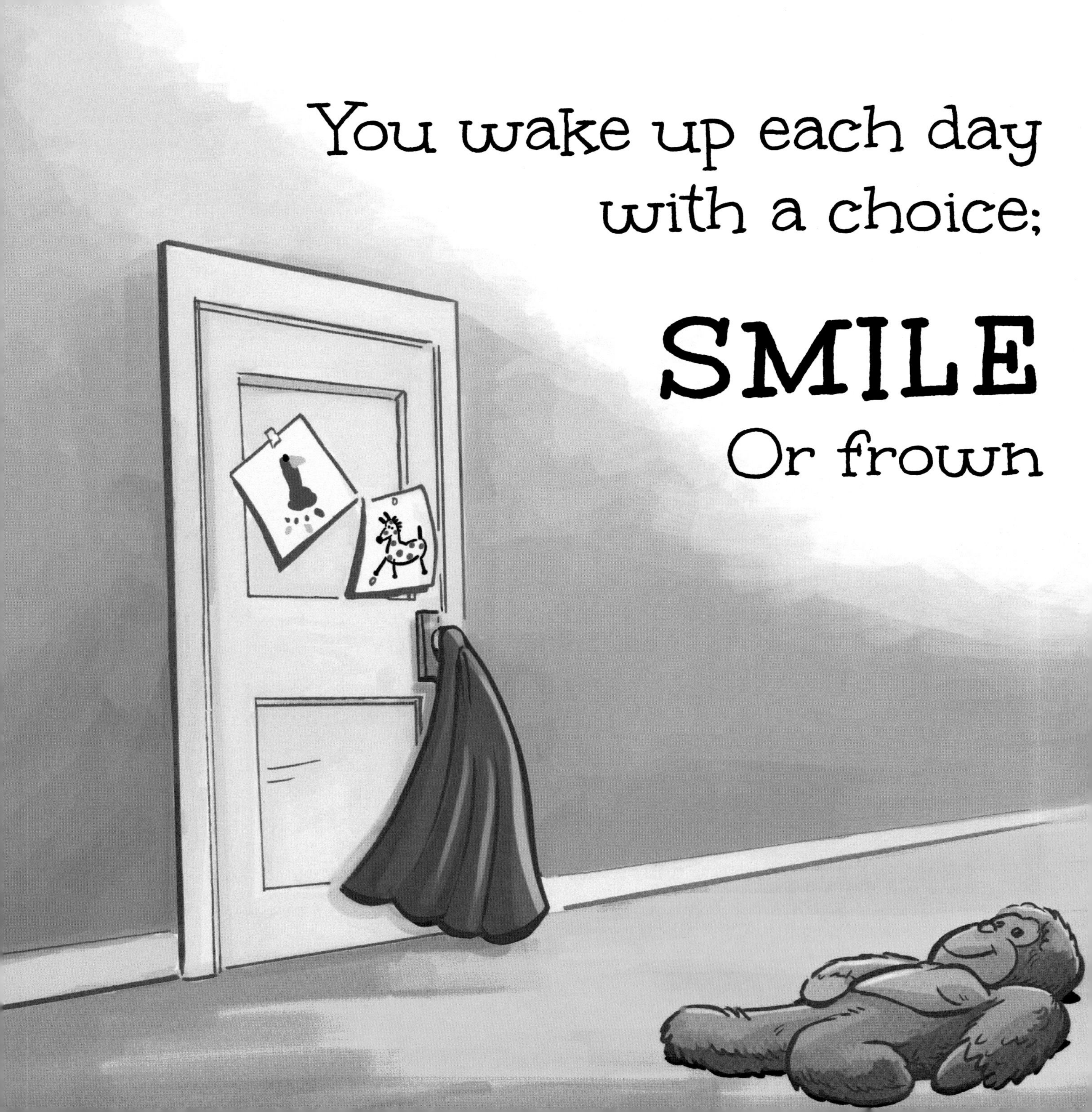

FACE THE WORLD

Or go back
to bed

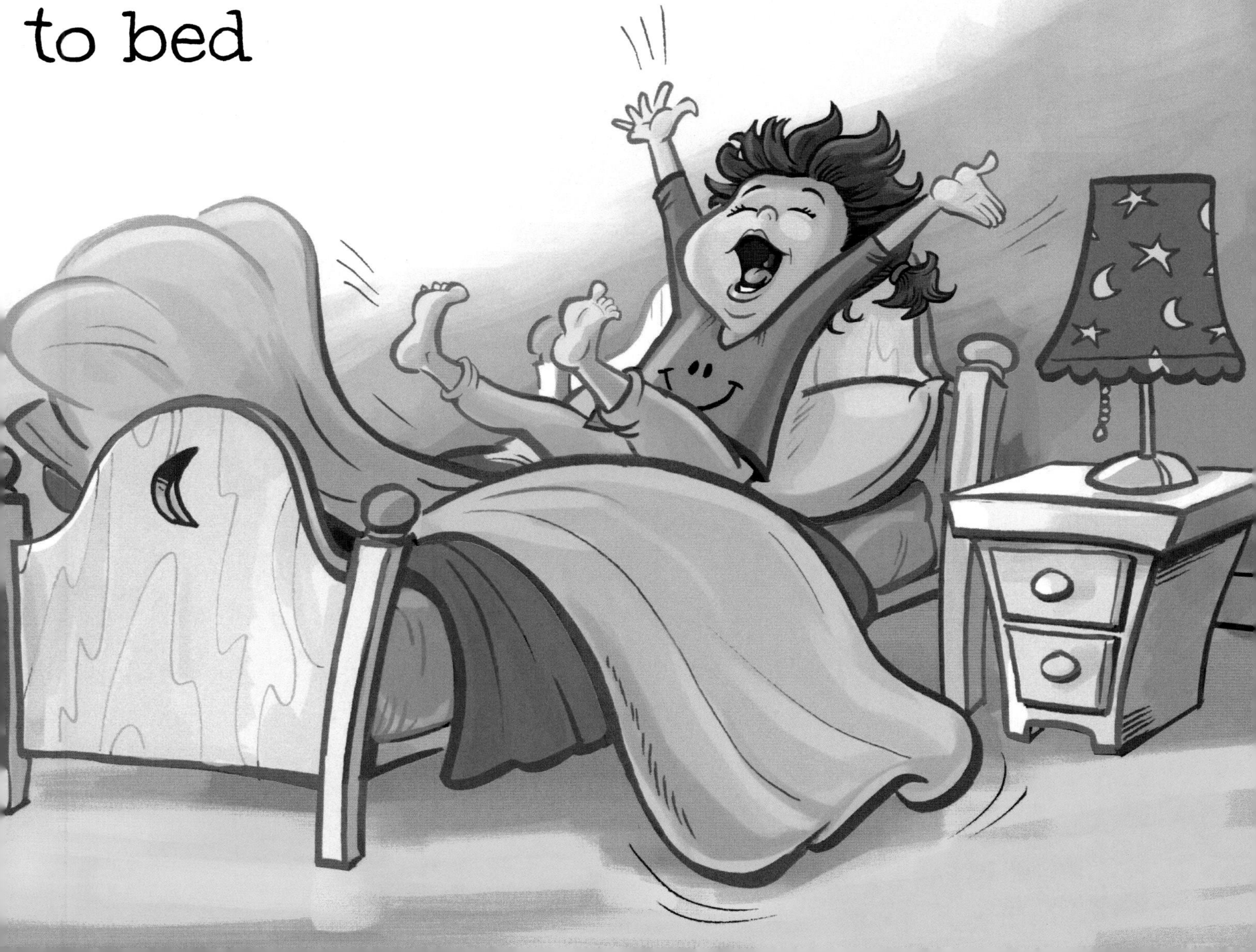

You may be one person among many but...

You are a **SUPERHERO**

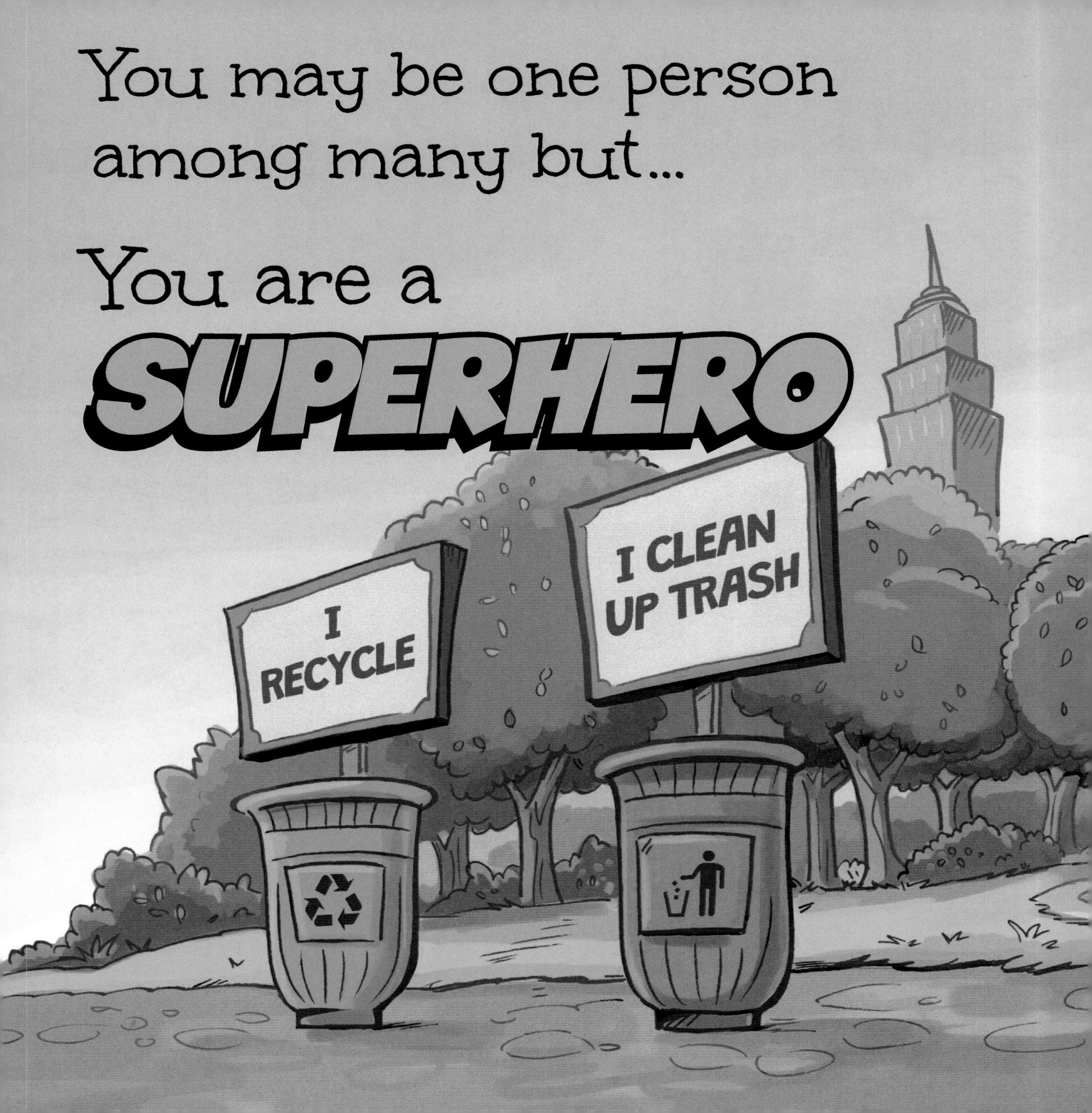
I RECYCLE
I CLEAN UP TRASH

You are IMPORTANT

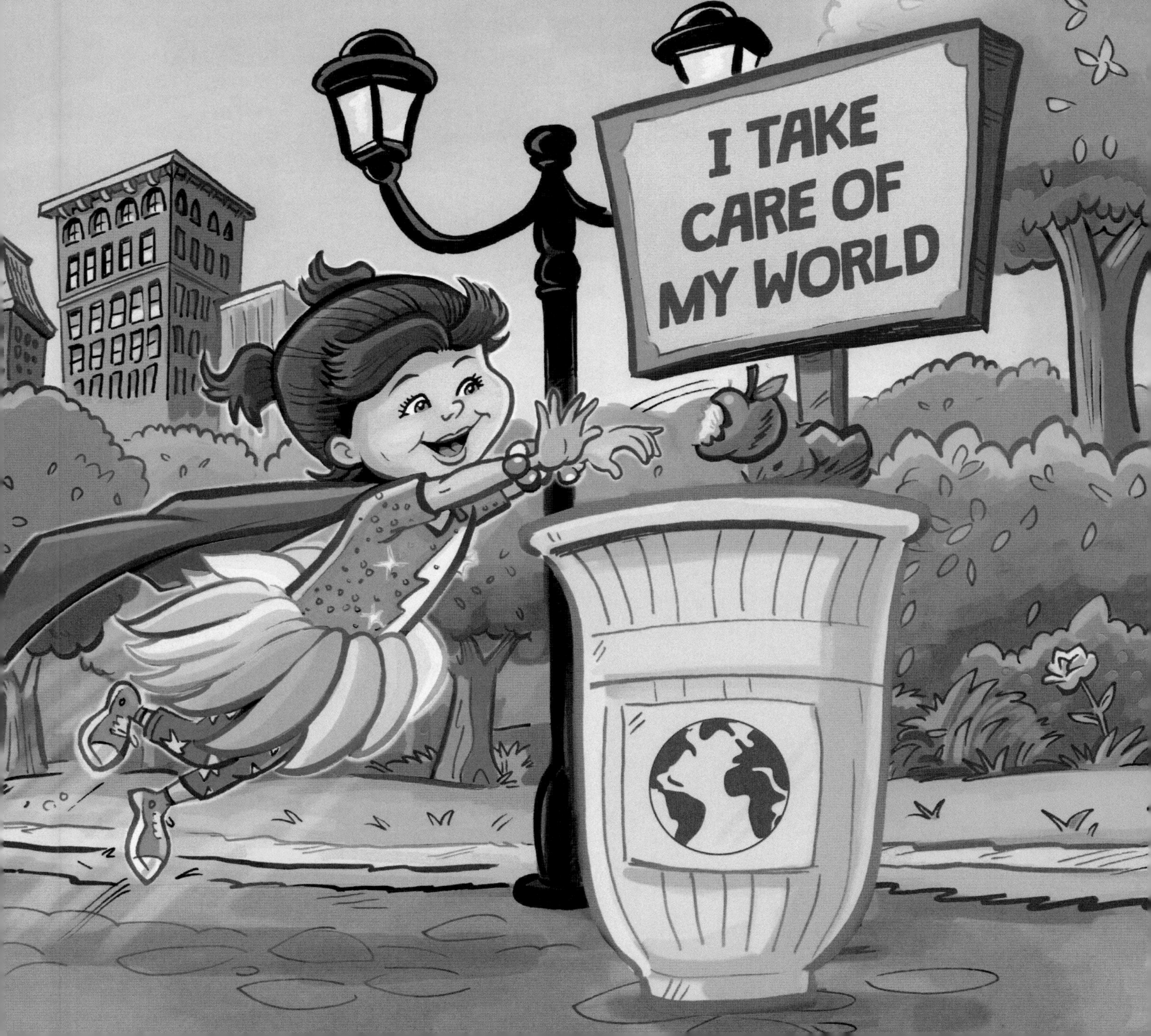
I TAKE
CARE OF
MY WORLD

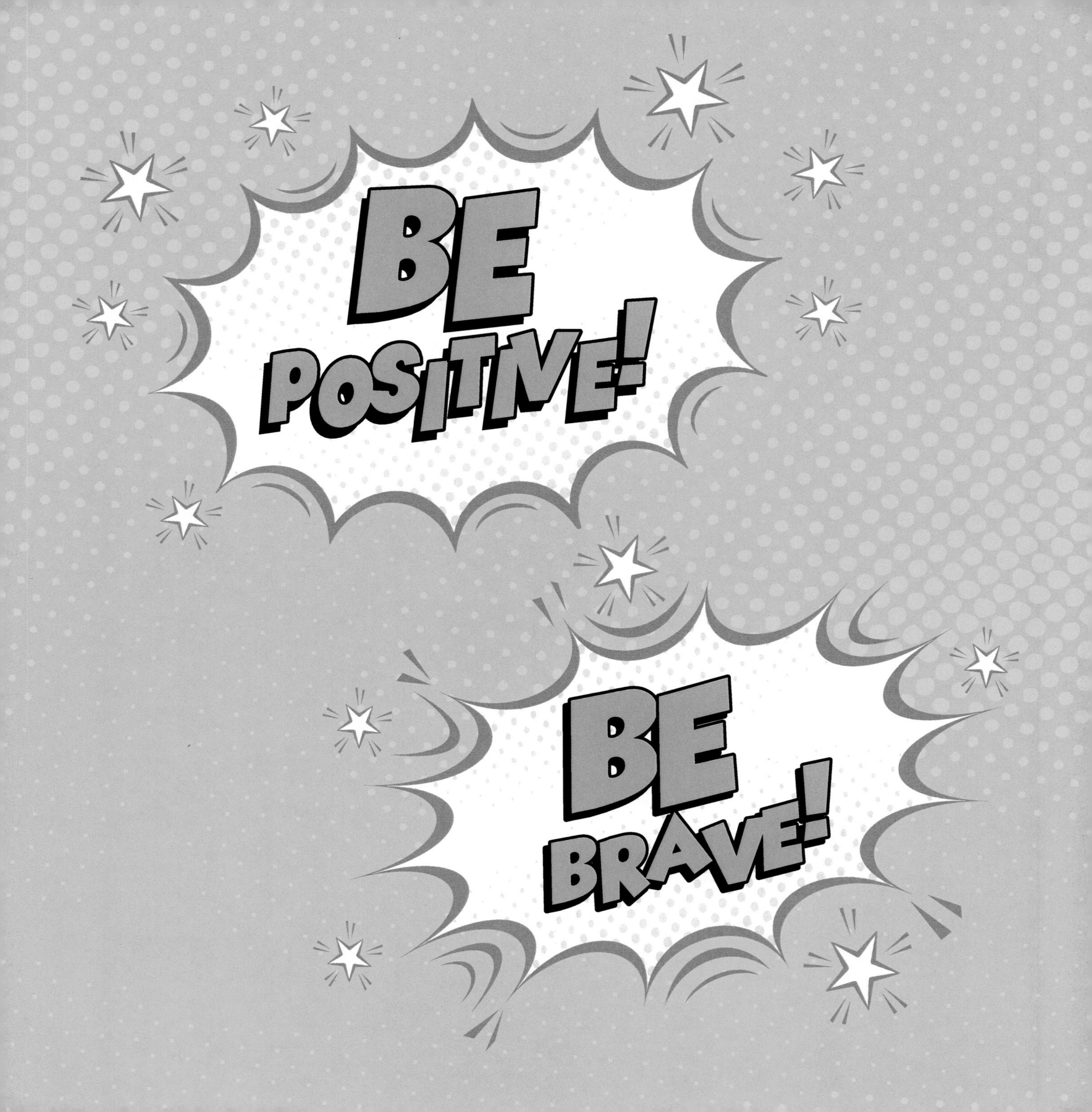
BE POSITIVE!
BE BRAVE!

BE RESPECTFUL!

BE YOUR BEST SELF!

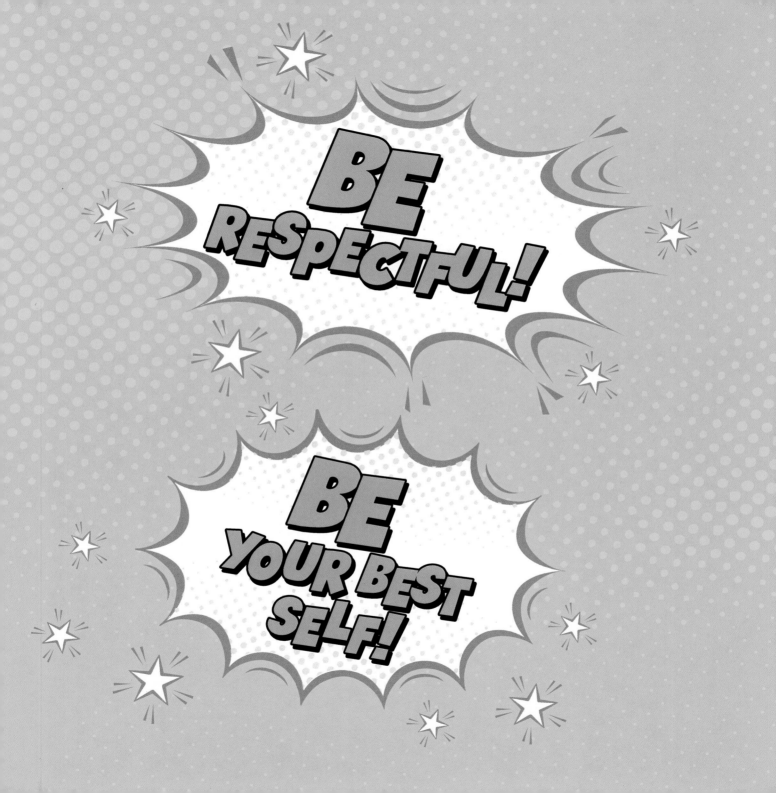

Choose wisely what you **SAY**

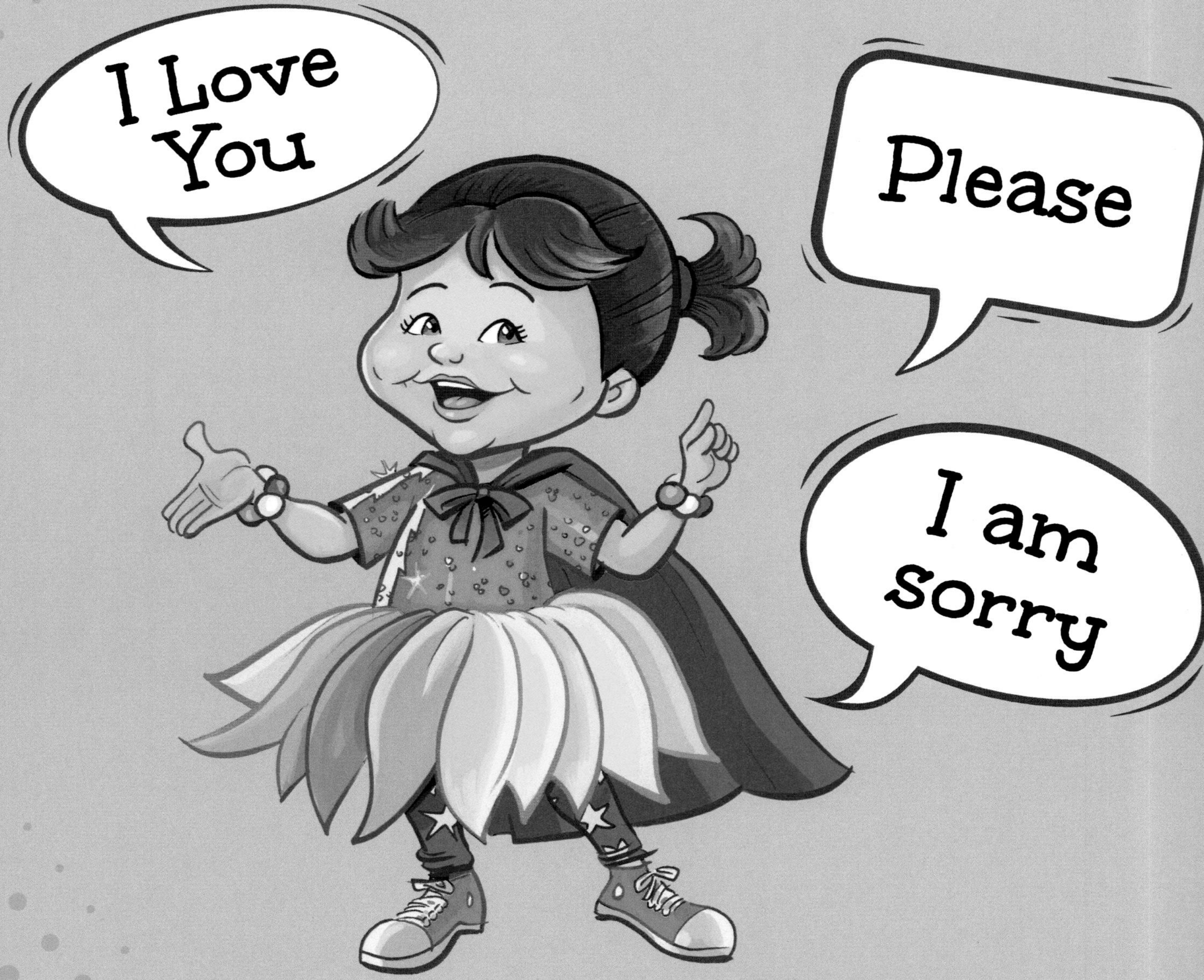
I Love You
Please
I am sorry

Because the **WORDS** of a

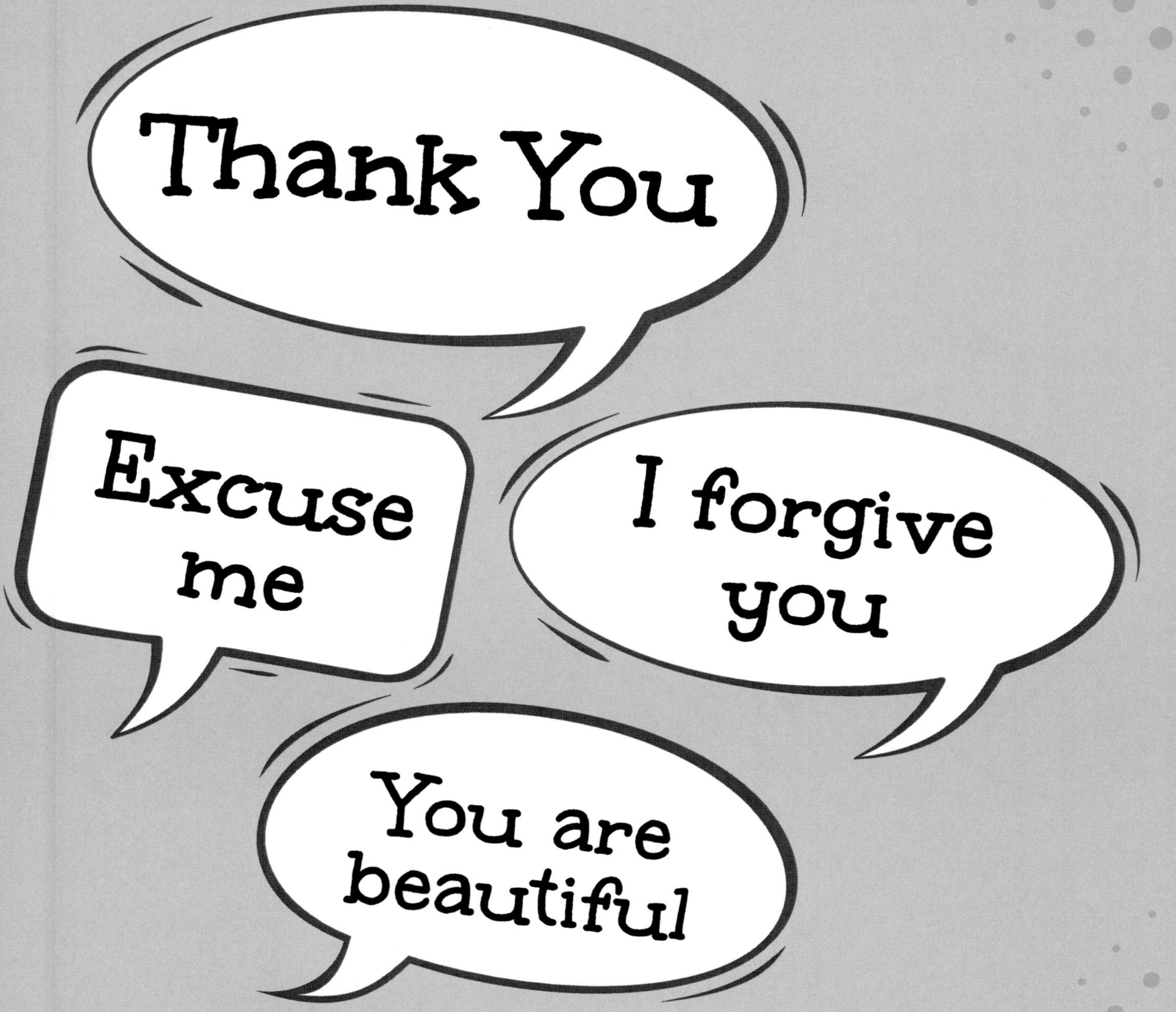
Thank You
Excuse me
I forgive you
You are beautiful

SUPERHERO are POWERFUL

Choose WISELY
what you do

Because the ACTIONS of a

SUPERHERO

can CHANGE THE WORLD

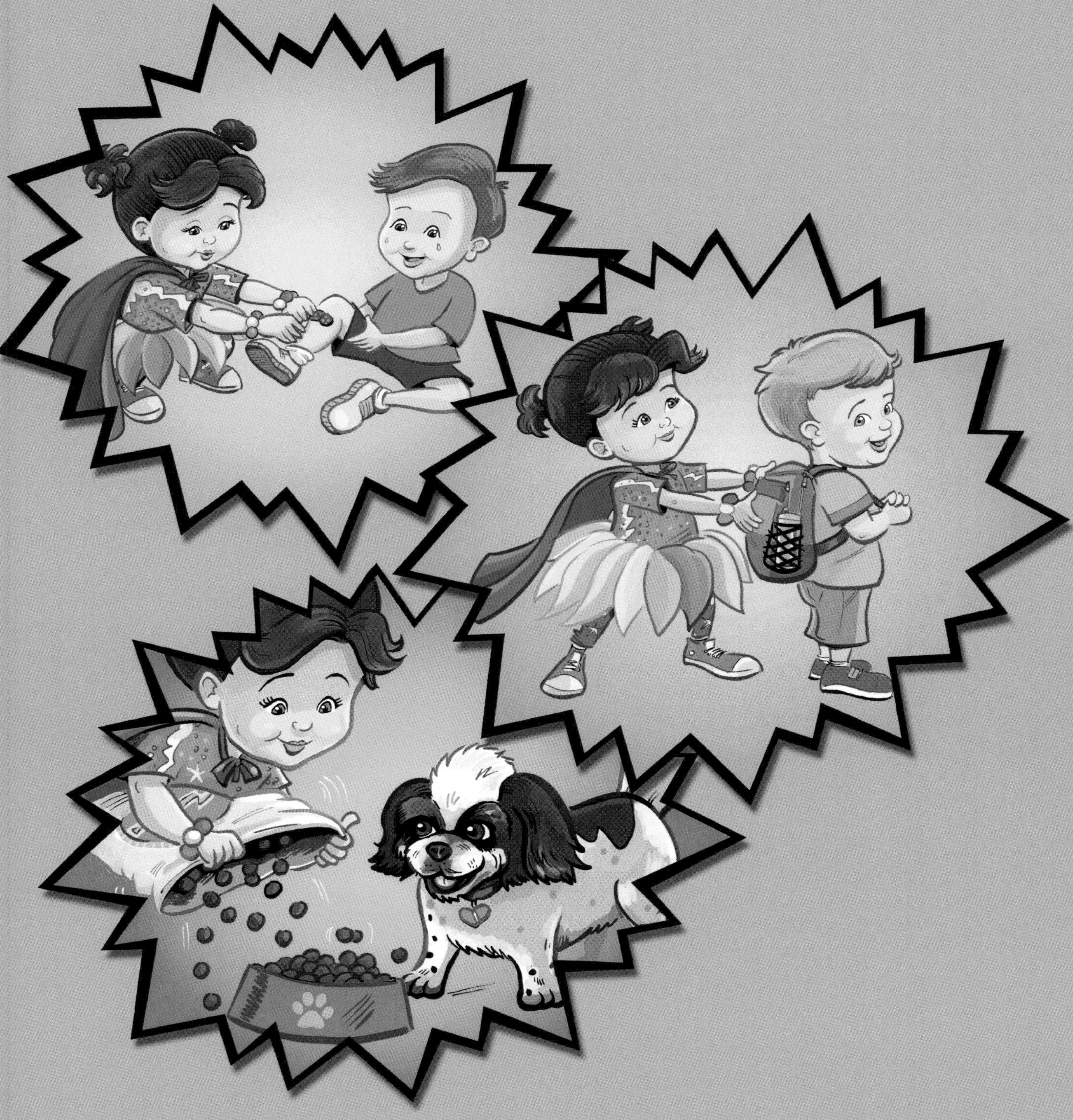

SUPERHEROES can be STRONG
But they are
GENTLE with their touch

SUPERHEROES can be tough
But they share
LOVE everywhere

SUPERHEROES leave the
world better than how
they found it

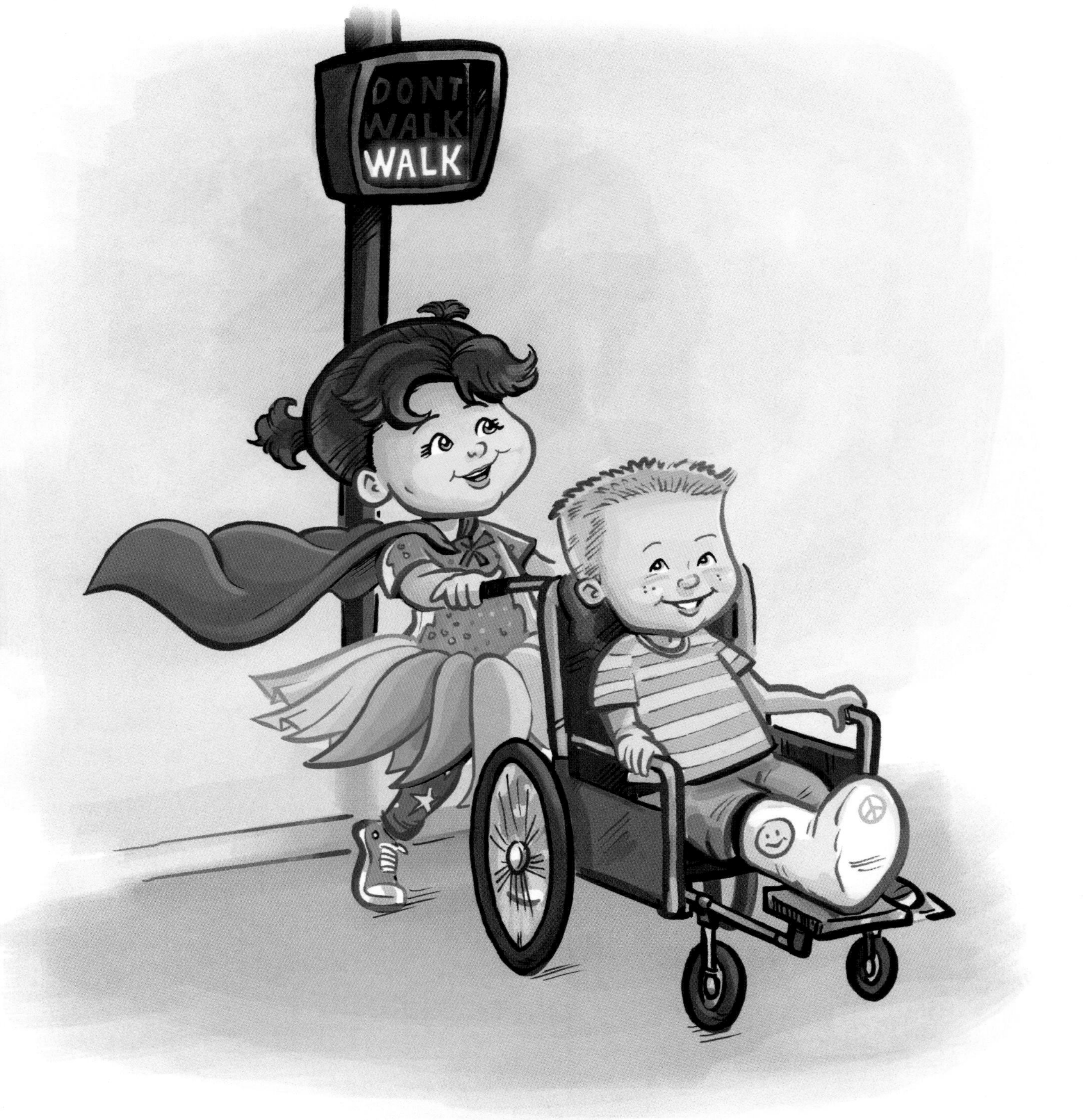
DONT
WALK
WALK

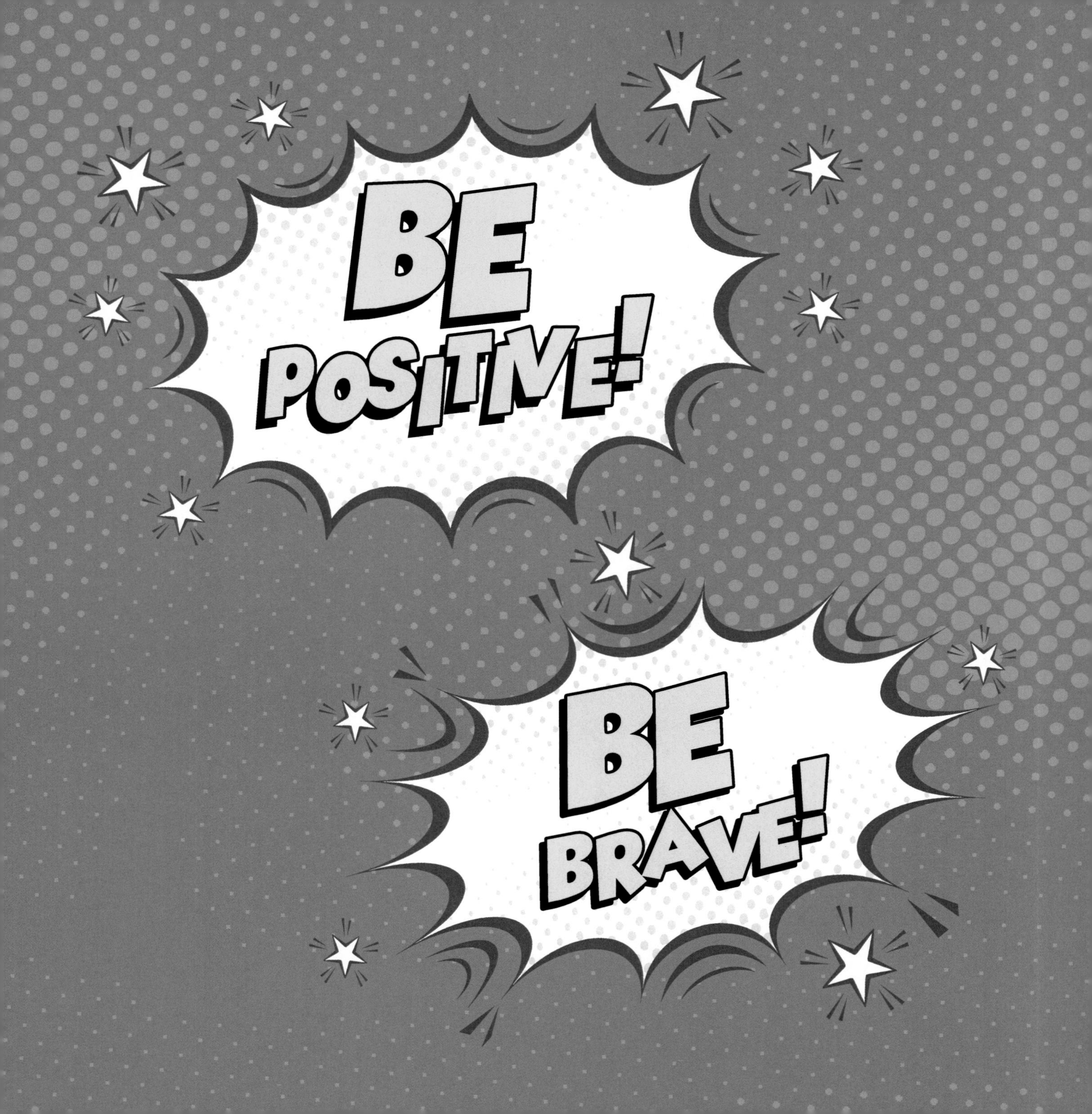
BE POSITIVE!
BE BRAVE!

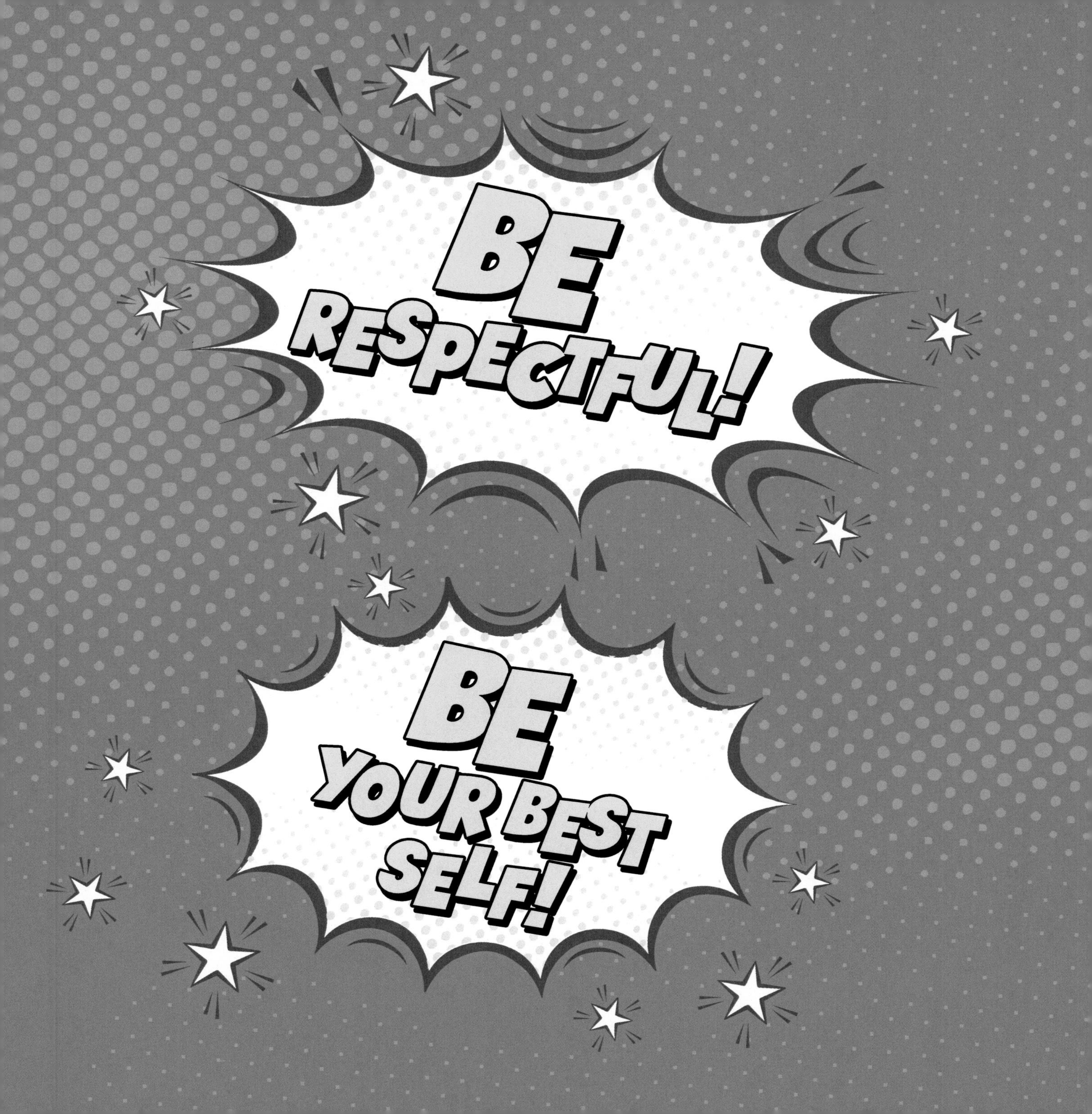
BE
RESPECTFUL!
BE
YOUR BEST
SELF!

PLANT
trees

CLEAN UP
your mess

HUG OTHERS and
make them **LAUGH**

Do your very
BEST

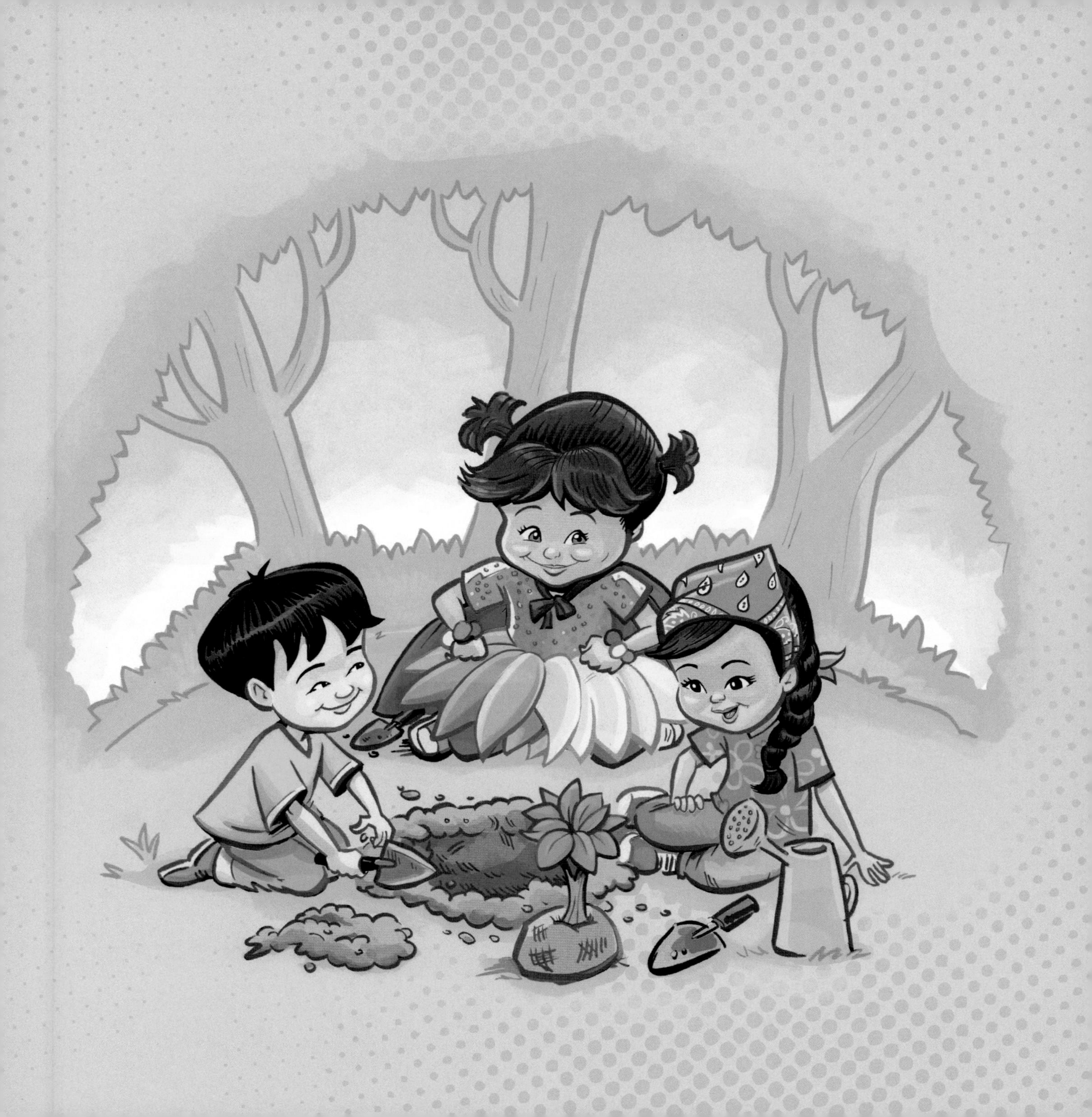

Being a
SUPERHERO
is quite a lot of work

YOU can do it
YOU can do
anything

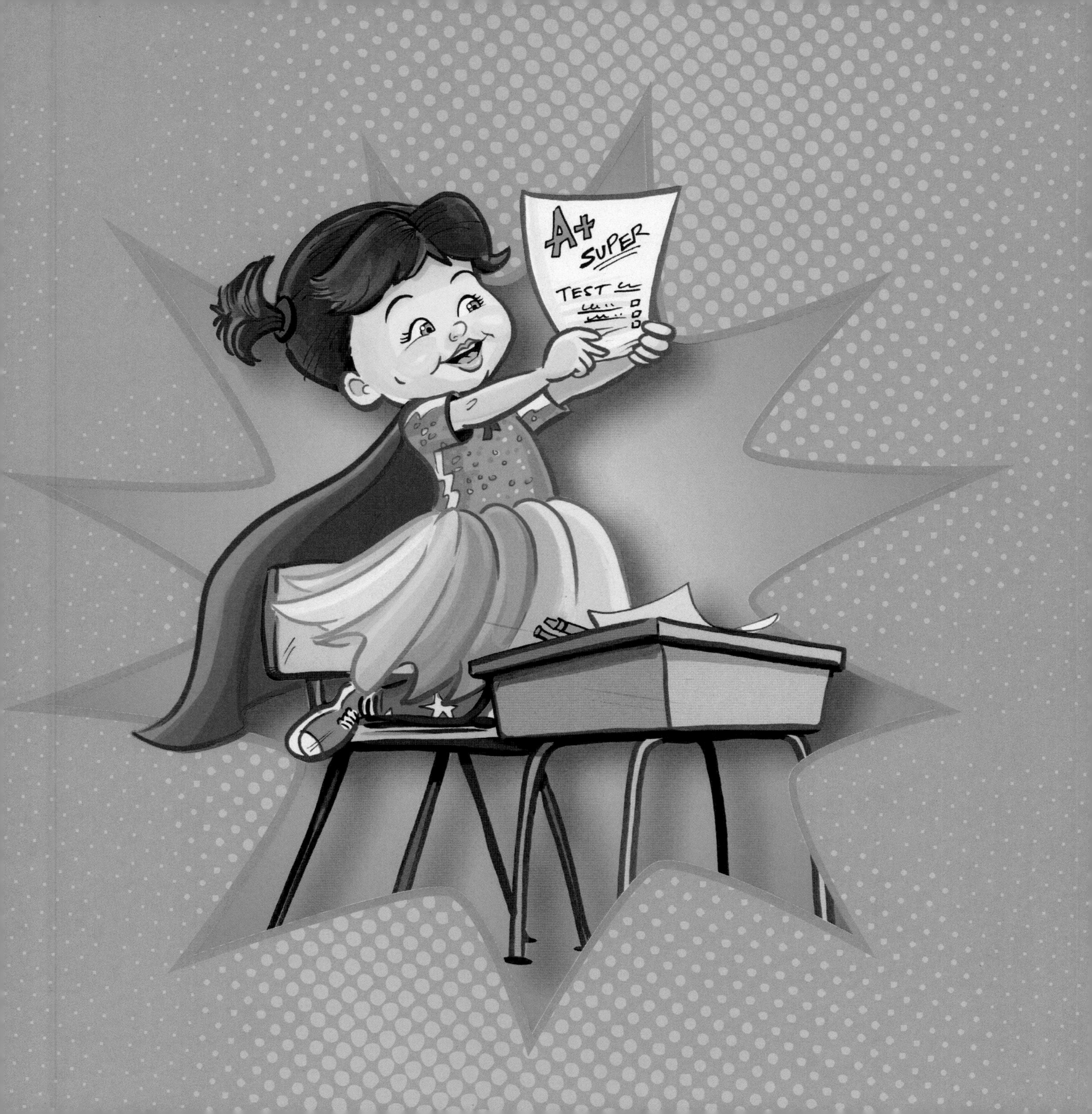
A+
SUPER
TEST

The world is so lucky
to have you in charge

You **WILL** make this
world a better place

Be the best
SUPERHERO
that you can be

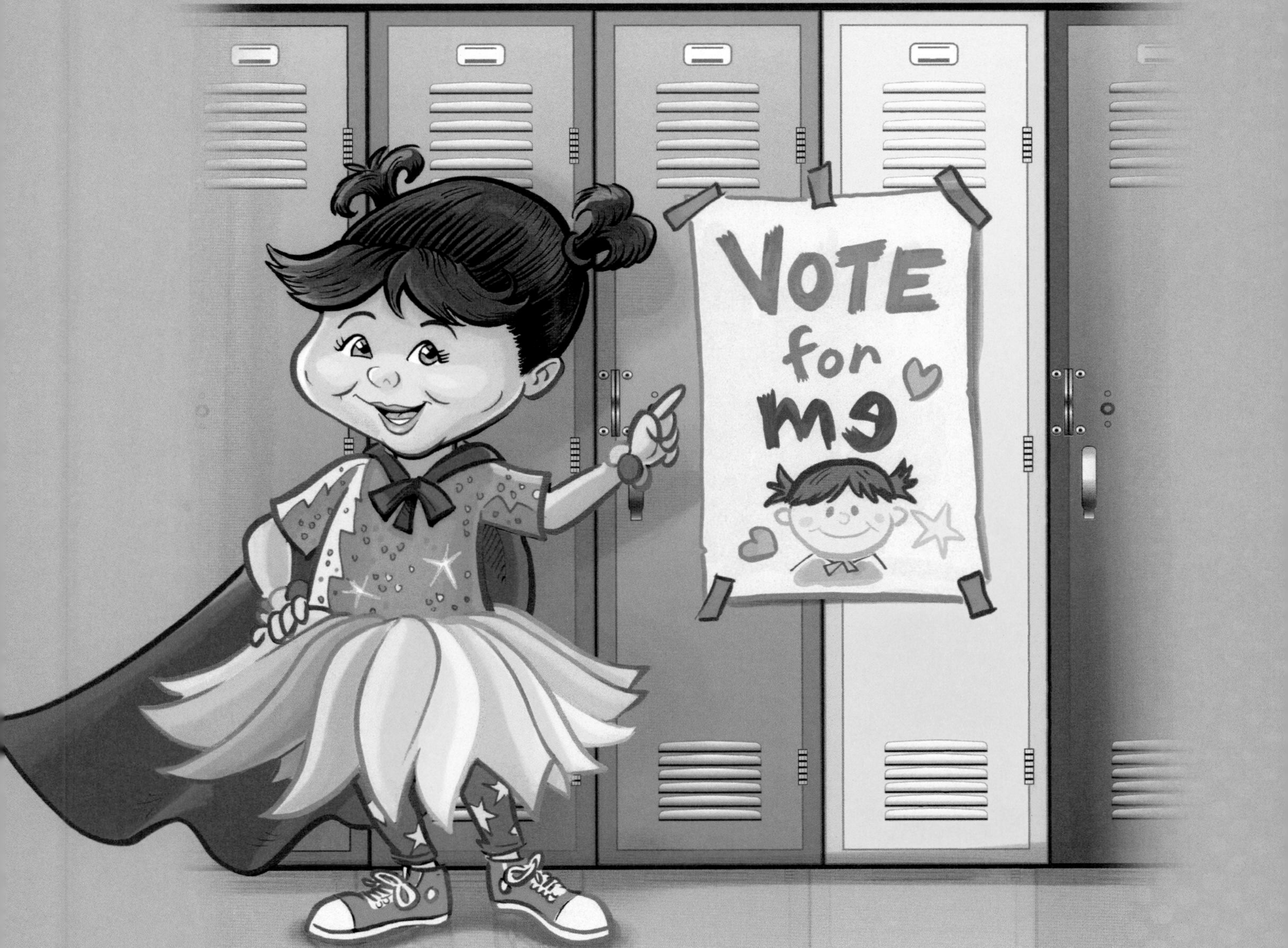
VOTE
for
me

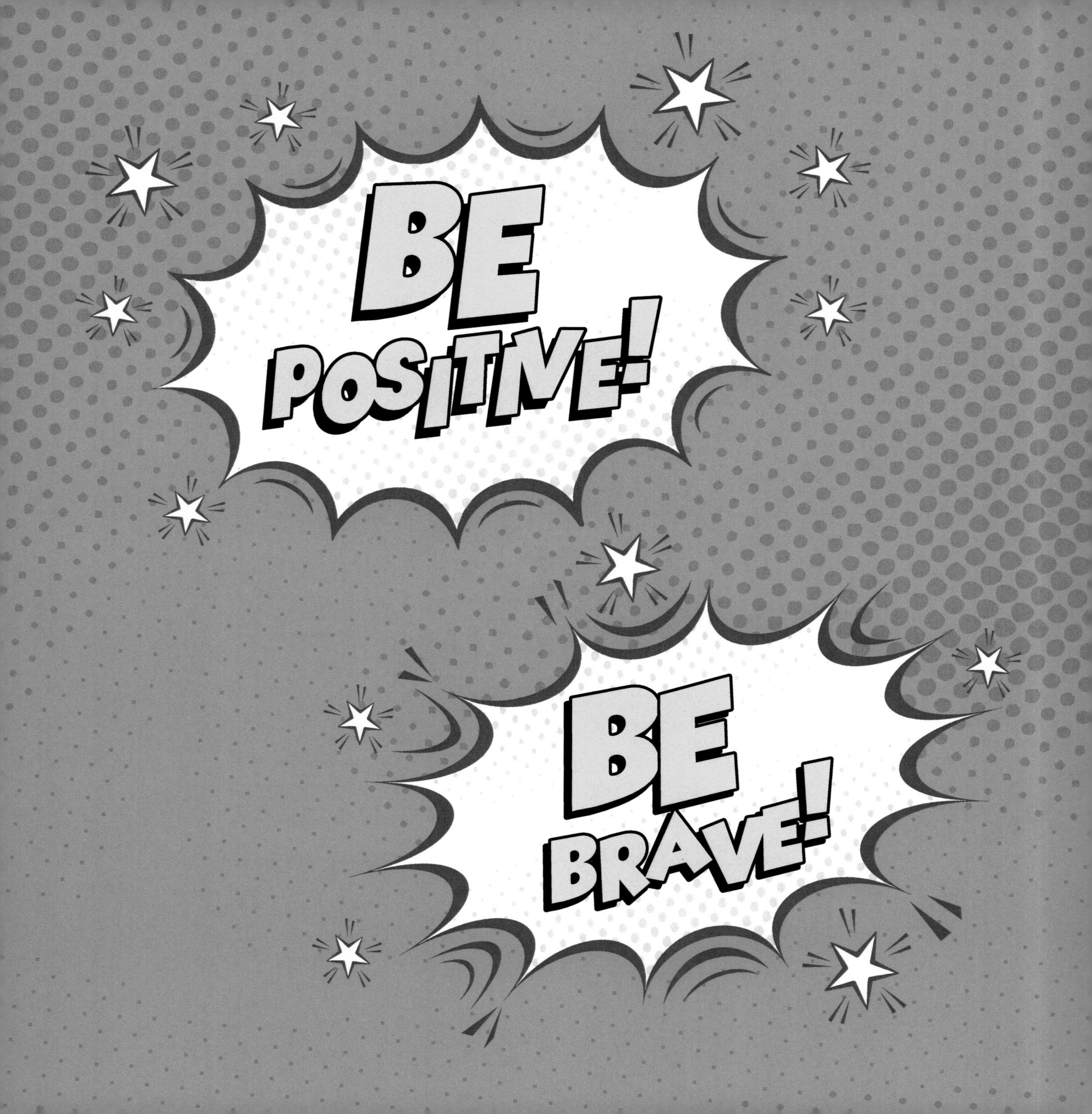
BE POSITIVE!
BE BRAVE!

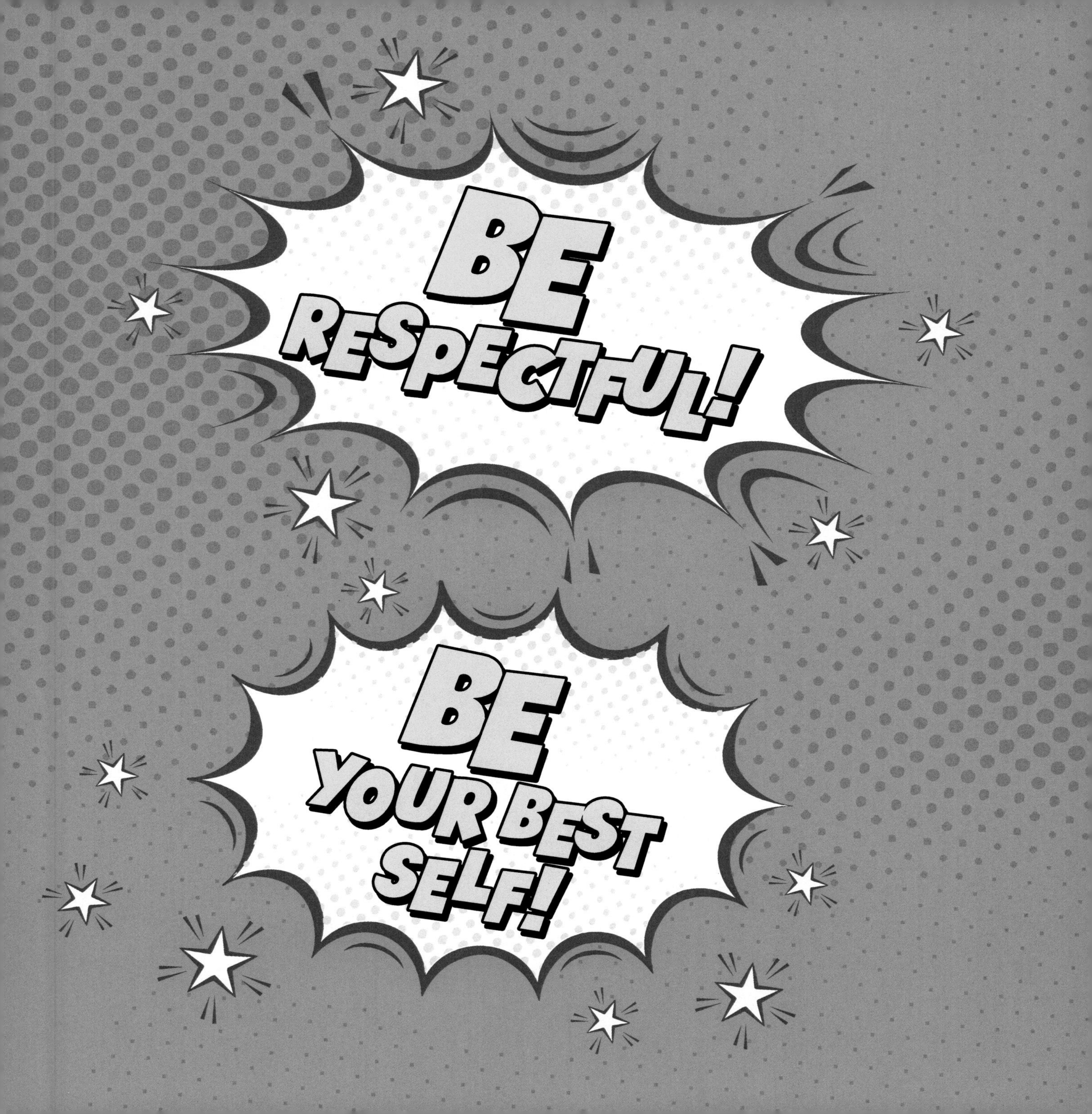
BE
RESPECTFUL!
BE
YOUR BEST
SELF!

Always be yourself

And be proud
of who you are

Every **SUPERHERO**
is UNIQUE

Every **SUPERHERO**
is BEAUTIFUL
in his or her own way

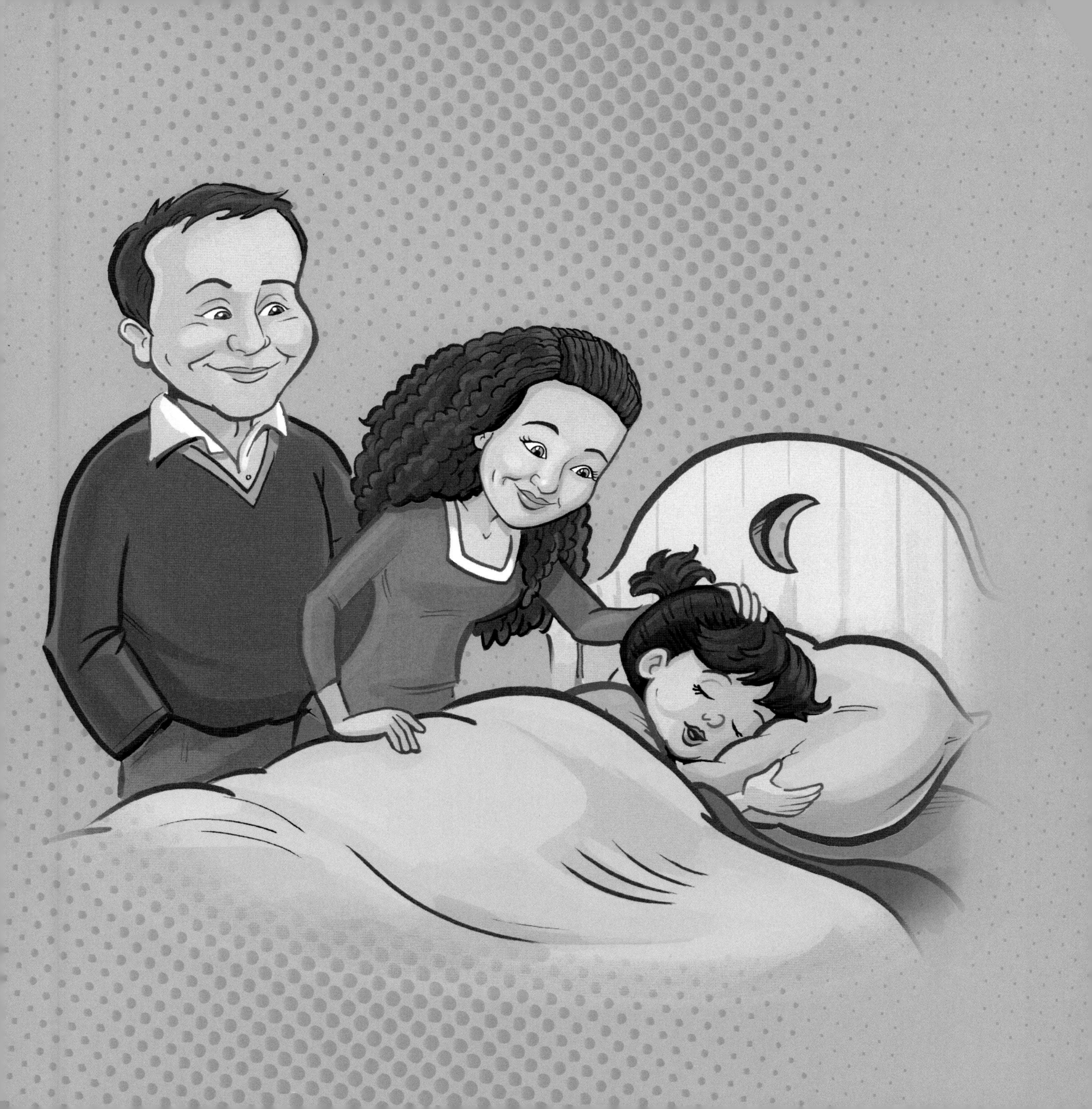

Inspiration & Discussion

Dear Parents and Educators,

    "You Are A Superhero" is a book that will inspire your children/students to do great things and to be the best version of themselves that they can be. This book allows them to see that a real superhero is not someone from the comic books or movies, but a person who makes kind choices and treats others with love and respect. It is my hope that through explanation and discussion, every child can realize that they are a REAL SUPERHERO!

    On the following pages, you will find discussion questions that can inspire and guide a conversation in your home or classroom. I feel that my purpose is to encourage these dialogues and hope that through deep discussion, every child can become aware of their potential in this world. We each have the ability to make a positive influence. It is my hope that through reading my books, and having the proper discussions, every child can go out into the world with confidence, kindness, respect, and positivity.

                    With love and gratitude,

                    Lauren Grabois Fischer

· Each day is a gift. What will you do to make the most of your gift that you've been given? How will you make today the best day that it can be?

· What does it mean to recycle? Why is it important that we recycle?

· Where does your garbage belong? Is it okay to spit your gum out the window when you are driving in the car? Is it okay to throw your garbage out of the car? What will the world look like if we all throw our garbage on the ground and not in a trash bin?

· Why should you be positive? How will this help you? Will your world be affected by your thoughts and perspective?

· What is a mantra? Why is it beneficial to repeat a positive saying to ourselves over and over? How can talking kindly to yourself help you be more confident and positive?

• What does it mean to be brave? Does being brave mean that I do scary things? Does being brave mean that I have to fight to get my way? No! Being brave can mean listening before talking, believing in yourself and those that you love, having the courage to take a risk if it can help you or another, and it means never giving up and always getting back up again even if things get tough.

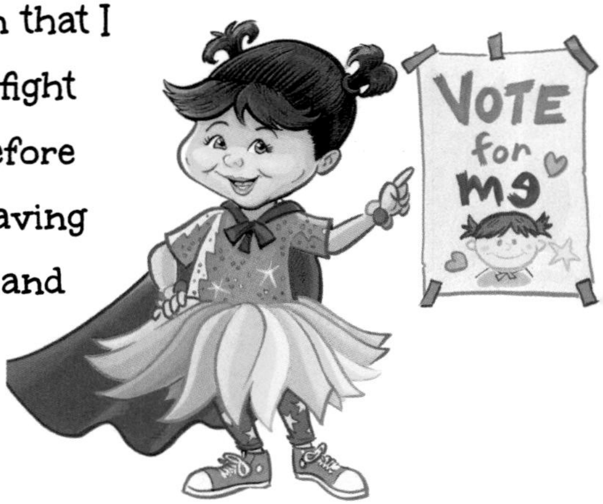
VOTE
for
me

• I repeated the mantra, "Be your best self!" What does this mean to you? How can you show the world your best version of you?

• Words are VERY powerful. Why should we use kind words when speaking to others? How do you feel when someone speaks kindly to you? How do you feel when someone speaks unkindly to you? Can it change the way your day goes? Make sure that you are the reason someone comes home smiling. Make sure that your words are making someone's day brighter and better.

• Your actions and choices are very powerful. Helping a person in need can create a "domino effect" and in turn can create a kindness thread. Your kind action can lead to someone else performing a kind action. What is something that you can do to help someone else?

· How can we treat animals kindly? Is it important to be respectful to all living things? If we see a beautiful flower, should we pick it or should we admire it and leave it alone? If we see a bird or a lizard, should we watch and learn about it from afar or come close and bother it?

· What do trees give us?
Why is it a good idea to plant trees?

· How can you leave the world better than it is? What can you do to make a positive change in this world?

· Setting goals for ourselves is very important. Always find something to dream about and work towards. Study hard for a test in school. Put effort into your book report and do lots of research. Focus and listen in class. What is your favorite subject in school? What is your favorite thing to learn about?

Activity Pages

· Mantras are a wonderful way to remind yourself to be positive. In this book, the words, **"Be Positive,"** **"Be Brave,"** **"Be Respectful,"** and **"Be Your Best Self"** are mantras that you repeated three times throughout the book. What are some mantras that you can repeat at home? Create four sentences that you will repeat to yourself daily. An example: I am kind. I am beautiful. I am healthy. I am worth it.

· How can you show respect for someone? List five ways to show them respect. When you are done writing, practice those kind actions on family and friends.

1. _____

2. _____

3. _____

4. _____

5. _____

· Find a friend and practice speaking kindly to each other. Your words are very

  powerful. Work together to come up with a list of ten beautiful things that you can

  say to someone else.

· **Gratitude List:** Use the lines below to write five things that you are grateful for.

  1._____

  2._____

  3._____

  4._____

  5._____

· The world is lucky to have you! Remember that as you go on your way. Think of

  four qualities that you have that will make the world a better place.

  1._____

  2._____

  3._____

  4._____

- Make it a goal of yours to help at least two people a day. Whether it is holding a door open for someone, saying "Bless you" when someone sneezes, helping someone pick up their backpack that fell, feeding your pets, or helping someone that is unable to do something on their own... Let that be your goal.

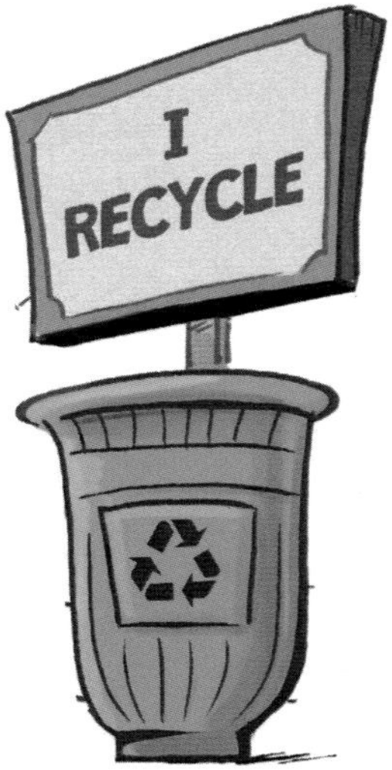
I
RECYCLE

- Start a recycling club in your home or classroom. If you do not already recycle, get your parents excited to begin this fun adventure. You can buy a special color bin for the items that you will recycle. If you are doing this in a school, maybe your class will be the first to inspire others to do the same. Collect empty bottles, paper, cardboard, and other items. You can offer many items to your art class in your school. They may be able to reuse these items for an art project.

· Start a Superhero club with your friends or classmates. Teach everyone what a REAL Superhero is! Someone who makes kind choices, is honest and caring, treats others and themselves with respect, and takes care of the world around them... that is a REAL SUPERHERO! Your club can do good things around your community on a monthly basis. Think of ways to make a positive change in our world.

Author's Note

Thank you so much for taking the time to read, "You Are A Superhero." I want to thank you personally for reading these words that I believe to be so powerful. I believe that we are all so special, and we all have an opportunity to better our world and our future. If each of us takes that responsibility seriously, there is no doubt that there will be more love and light in this world. I want to empower you to be the real superhero that you are. Make a change in your community. Make a change in your state. Stand up for what you know is right and what you believe in. Be accepting, kind, and respectful to all living beings and leave a sprinkle of your positive energy wherever you go. You are the best SUPERHERO, and I am so thankful for each of you!

With love and gratitude,

Lauren Grabois Fischer

Made in the USA
Columbia, SC
11 October 2020